The African elephant is the largest animal that lives on land. It is often said to be more fierce than the Indian elephant, but the African elephant is really a very gentle creature. When accompanied by its baby, the elephant will chase away dangerous animals, but it will almost never attack.

Elephants usually eat leaves and tree bark. They share their feeding ground with zebras, gnus, and Thomson gazelles but since each eats its own particular kind of plants, they all get along with one another. Giraffes, too, are often nearby, and cattle egrets may walk about at the elephants' feet. Elephants are said to live to the age of about sixty.

ELEPHANT CROSSING

written and illustrated by *Toshi Yoshida*

PHILOMEL BOOKS · NEW YORK

Under a hot African sun, eleven elephants gather to form a herd. A very wise and brave great-grandmother elephant leads them. Among the herd are a baby girl elephant and a slightly bigger boy elephant.

As the day grows warmer, great-grandmother elephant sets off,
leading the other elephants toward a forest where many delicious
leaves grow. Zebras graze along the way.

Across the plain, three young lions move slowly toward the zebras.
As big sister lion springs to attack, the zebras begin to run.

The zebras race behind the herd, but the elephants continue along their way.

One big male zebra does not run. He stands alert, as if ready to fight.
The three young lions creep closer and closer.

Suddenly the male zebra dashes away, escaping with the other zebras behind the elephant herd. Now the elephants find themselves face to face with the young lions. Brave great-grandmother elephant boldly charges them.

The fully grown African elephant is one of the strongest animals on land. But an adult elephant never knows when one of the baby elephants may be attacked by a lion or a leopard.

Great-grandmother elephant is always on guard. Nearby, cattle egrets peacefully eat grasshoppers.

But there are some things even fully grown elephants can not
guard against.

When great-grandmother elephant was just a baby she was toddling
along one day by her mother's side.

Suddenly, from the sky behind them, a giant cloud appeared and
moved toward them.

Making an eerie noise, the strange cloud came closer and closer. And then, before they knew it, the air was filled with swarms of insects!

The elephants flapped their ears and swung their trunks, but nothing helped.

Swarm upon swarm of desert grasshoppers swirled and settled
around the elephants, looking for food.

Trees that had grown green and leafy were quickly cropped short. In no time at all, all the grass and leaves were gone.

Frightened, the giraffes began to run. Even the cattle egrets, who
usually eat grasshoppers, flew away to escape them.

The little girl elephant ran as fast as she could, staying close beside her mother.

The elephants ran blindly through the cloud of insects. But the more they ran, the thicker the cloud of grasshoppers grew.

The little girl elephant began to grow tired. But she couldn't leave her mother's side or she would get lost. Desperately, she grasped her mother's tail with her trunk.

Finally, the desert grasshoppers turned away. The African elephants
looked around them. The grass and the leaves and everything green
had all been eaten up. The plain had become like a desert.

Some of the elephants must have gotten lost trying to escape the swarms of grasshoppers. Of the larger herd, there now remained only seven.

The African elephants set out in search of food. The brown, bare plain seemed to spread across the land forever. The elephants could not find green grass anywhere.

The long, hot journey stretched on and on. Tired and hungry, the little girl elephant stayed close to her mother.

The African elephants walked on for many days. Finally they came
upon a great, green forest. Mother and baby girl elephant ate all the
green leaves they could.

Here there were no dreadful swarms of grasshoppers. Everything smelled wonderfully of leaves and grass.

Over the years the fear of that long-ago time has remained with great-grandmother elephant. But in the forest there are no terrible swarms of grasshoppers.

And there are lots of leaves and grass. Great-grandmother trumpets
contentedly. Today there is only peace.

Sometimes the grasshopper population in a certain area will suddenly begin to grow. At such times, their color, shape, and nature change completely and they fly like a cloud, searching for food. They have even been known to leave Africa and fly to Asia and Europe. After the grasshoppers have passed through, leaves, grass, and crops are all eaten up. It is said that of the grasshopper family, the desert grasshopper causes the most damage of all.

Text and illustrations copyright © 1984 by Toshi Yoshida.
American text copyright © 1989 by Philomel Books.
All rights reserved. Published in the United States by
Philomel Books, a division of The Putnam & Grosset Group,
200 Madison Avenue, New York, NY 10016.
Published simultaneously in Canada.
Originally published under the title *Omoide*
by Fukutake Publishing Co., Ltd., Tokyo, Japan.
Based on an English translation by Susan Matsui.
English translation rights arranged with
Fukutake Publishing Co., Ltd. through Japan Foreign Rights Centre.
Printed in Hong Kong by South China Printing Co. (1988) Ltd.
Designed by Christy Hale.

Library of Congress Cataloging-in-Publication Data   Yoshida, Toshi, 1911– Elephant crossing/written and illustrated by Toshi Yoshida. p. cm. Summary: Describes the perils faced by a herd of African elephants in the course of their daily lives. ISBN 0-399-21745-2: 1. African elephant—Juvenile literature. [1. Elephants.] I. Title. QL737.P98Y67 1989   599.6′1—dc19   88-34877 CIP AC
First Impression.

DATE			
		✓	